Waiting for Benjamin

A Story about Autism

Alexandra Jessup Altman   Illustrated by Susan Keeter

Albert Whitman & Company, Morton Grove, Illinois

For Philip and Elias.—A.J.A.

To Daniel and Kaden, who helped, and to Marsha Tankersley Tucker,
Glynn County, Georgia, Special Education Teacher of the Year
and awesome grandma.—S.K.

Library of Congress Cataloging-in-Publication Data

Altman, Alexandra.
Waiting for Benjamin : a story about autism / by Alexandra Jessup Altman ; illustrated by Susan Keeter.
p. cm.
Summary: Alexander experiences feelings of disappointment, anger, embarrassment, and jealousy
when his younger brother is diagnosed with autism.
ISBN 978-0-8075-7364-8 (hardcover)
[1. Autism—Fiction. 2. Brothers—Fiction.] I. Keeter, Susan, ill. II. Title.
PZ7.A46387Wai 2008 [E]—dc22 2007024248

The design is by Carol Gildar.

For more information about Albert Whitman & Company,
please visit our web site at www.albertwhitman.com.

NOTE

    While working with children with autism and their families, I've observed that siblings face many emotional challenges. Some of these are similar to what their parents experience: disappointment, frustration, embarrassment, and uncertainty. Affection given is not always tolerated or reciprocated. The child with autism may lack language, making play a struggle. He or she may act conspicuously in public, bringing unwanted attention. But most difficult for many siblings of children with autism is the huge diversion of parental and professional resources towards the child with the diagnosis. The typical child can find him or herself competing for time and attention, despite earnest efforts by parents to compensate. Children may have angry or unkind thoughts toward their siblings with autism, or an overall sense that "it's not fair," but feel too guilty to reveal their feelings.

    Parents have a unique opportunity to explore these difficult feelings through reading books with their children. I hope that *Waiting for Benjamin* will provide just such an opportunity. By describing for both parents and children some of the challenging emotional situations that occur, it can help them share their own perceptions and recollections, not only about what is painful in family life but about what is humorous and tender as well. Children can discover, as Alexander did, that as people grow, life changes, and friendships bloom in unexpected places.

Alexandra Jessup Altman
Senior Interventionist
Autism Spectrum Program
HowardCenter for Human Services
Burlington, Vermont

My name is Alexander and I was born first. Then came Benjamin. We live in a stone house with Mom and Dad.

After Benjamin's second birthday we all waited for him to talk, but he didn't say any words. He just wiggled his fingers and rocked. One day I gave him my favorite bear, but he only wanted to look at the bumpy place on the wall.

"Grrr," I said, because now I felt angry. "My bear is going to bite you." My bear growled hard into Benjamin's face. Mom said, "That is *not* okay, Alexander."

I even showed him my pirate
ship, but he didn't look at all.
Then I was sad *and* mad.

Benjamin mostly just rocks on a wobbly stool in the living room, wiggling his fingers. He does this practically all day. If I call his name, he doesn't move. Once I shouted at him, "Are you deaf?"

When my friend Zach said, "That kid is a wacko," I wished I had no brother.

Another day I made a huge castle with blocks and blankets and pillows. I made a flag with a shield on it. I really wanted someone to play with me. It was the best thing I ever built.

"Ben, look. Come play knights. You can have my silver sword."
I put it right into his hand, but he didn't hold on at all. I had
to pull him over to the castle because I don't think he understands
English. He took my flag and threw it up in the air. I think he just
wanted to see it fall. I grabbed it back and he went away.

He never does anything I want.

One morning Mom and Dad took Benjamin to the doctor. That night, after I got ready for bed, they told me about it. The doctor said the reason Benjamin wasn't talking and playing with me was because he has something called autism.

"Part of his brain is different, and that makes it hard for Benjamin to listen and to look at us," said Mom. Dad told me no one knows why some kids have autism, but that many scientists are trying to figure it out.

"When is he going to stop just wiggling and start playing with me?" I asked. Mom said some people were going to start coming to our house to teach Benjamin to listen and talk and play.

I was glad. I wanted him to grow up faster.

Mom told me some more things in the morning. She said the doctor thought that when Benjamin wiggled his fingers, it felt so good to him he didn't hear us. I went to the backyard and tried wiggling my fingers to see what the feeling was, but it didn't feel that good to me.

When Benjamin looks so long into the air, I wonder
what he sees? Is it better than here? Are there people?

One morning two ladies knocked at the front door. Mom and
Dad both went to open it. Mom said to me, "Say hello to Benjamin's
new teachers."

"This is Alexander, Benjamin's brother," Dad told them.

The teachers are Julie and Emma. When they come to work and
play with Benjamin, they bring lots of toys. I heard a dinging bell
once and saw a flashing rocket. Julie and Emma always say, "Hi, guy,"
but they don't show me what they're hiding in the carry bags, and
they never say, "Want to come down with us for a while?"

When Benjamin and Julie go into the basement, Mom says, "Alexander, that door stays closed." But one time I went down the stairs and peeked in. I saw Benjamin and Julie sitting at the little play table, but they didn't see me.

When Julie said, "Look at me," and Benjamin looked, he got a big hug. When Julie said, "What is it? Say 'blue ball,'" and Benjamin said, "buh, buh, blue," he got a hug and a tiger animal cracker.

I wanted it to be my turn. Then I would say everything perfectly, and Julie would smile and give me a special reward.

I found Mom and Dad in the family room. Mom was reading a book and Dad had his newspaper. "I know the names of all the things in the world," I told them.

Dad said, "That would be a lot of names," but he didn't even look at me.

Mom said, "Are you getting hungry for lunch?" I don't think she was listening.

It's not fair! When Benjamin makes any sounds, Mom and Dad go right over to him.

I stomped upstairs. I was mad and felt like making a mess.
I walked into Benjamin's room and saw his dumb moon-and-stars
water cup by his bed. He always cries if it isn't exactly in the middle
of the table when Mom tucks him in. I went over to it and pushed it
a little. It fell off the edge, and water spilled onto Benjamin's pillow.

Later Dad asked, "Alexander, why is Benjamin's pillow all wet?"
I told him, "Benjamin gets lots of prizes every day."

"Alexander," Dad said, "you know that Benjamin has to hear words
many times to learn them. The little prizes help him do hard things.
I wonder if you were feeling angry up in Benjamin's room?"

"Yes," I said. "I just want something special for me to have."

Then Dad had an idea. "What if you and I make a tent in the
backyard with some rope and a tarp? We could sleep out tonight."

I was surprised about this idea, then I wanted to do it.
We worked a long time until Dad said, "Now it's snug."
When we were going to sleep, Dad said, "Maybe one
day Benjamin will do this with us."
I said, "Maybe," but I didn't think so.

That night I had a dream, and I told Mom about it in the morning.

"I dreamed I was a dolphin swimming in a dark blue sea. First I was alone, but then another dolphin came. I jumped out of the water and into the air and so did he. It was Benjamin. He wanted to follow me."

Mom smiled and gave me a kiss. "I love you. You are my dreamer."

Benjamin has been working with Julie and Emma for a very
long time now. I moved to the 2/3 class in school. A new boy, Emory,
is my friend. I bike to his house after school and we work on our
hidden fort. His garden shed is our headquarters.

We put flashlights and
gum in a box under a stone.
We invented a secret code,
tapping drumsticks on the tin roof;
then we made up our own language.
Emory calls me "Hendrikamacoti."
I named him "Materatali."

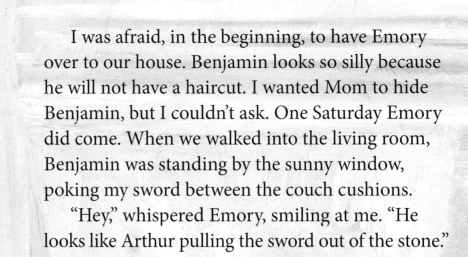

I was afraid, in the beginning, to have Emory over to our house. Benjamin looks so silly because he will not have a haircut. I wanted Mom to hide Benjamin, but I couldn't ask. One Saturday Emory did come. When we walked into the living room, Benjamin was standing by the sunny window, poking my sword between the couch cushions.

"Hey," whispered Emory, smiling at me. "He looks like Arthur pulling the sword out of the stone."

I smiled, too, because Emory was right.

Sunday night Benjamin
played fast-food restaurant with me.
He listened to my order when I drove
up to his window. He had a golden crown
on his head. He gave me a big plate of
plastic food: french fries on top of cake on
top of spaghetti.

I said, "Thank you, Your Majesty, for my
crazy meal." Benjamin bowed, and we both fell
down laughing.

The next morning Benjamin surprised Mom at breakfast when he said, "Benjamin likes toast. Benjamin does not like eggs." I got excited and said, "Benjamin, say 'Alexander.'"

"Zander," he said. I tried to get him to say the "Alex-an" part, but he only said "Zander" and touched my ear.

I decided I liked that funny, short name.

I don't feel so sad and mad anymore.
Now my brother is my friend. But
when Benjamin looks far away,
I still wonder what he is seeing.
One day I am going
to ask him.